# Ja Bird Feeder

written by Barbara Kanninen

illustrated by Kathy O'Malley

KAEDEN BOOKS™

The children came inside after recess.

"Look!" said Jake. "Peanut butter!"

"Yummy," said Robert, grabbing a spoon.

"Hey, put that down!" said Maria. "Can't you see it's for a project? We're going to make bird feeders, aren't we, Mrs. Stark? I can tell because of the bird seed."

"That's right, Maria," said Mrs. Stark. "Please take your seats so we can get started." She handed out the instructions.

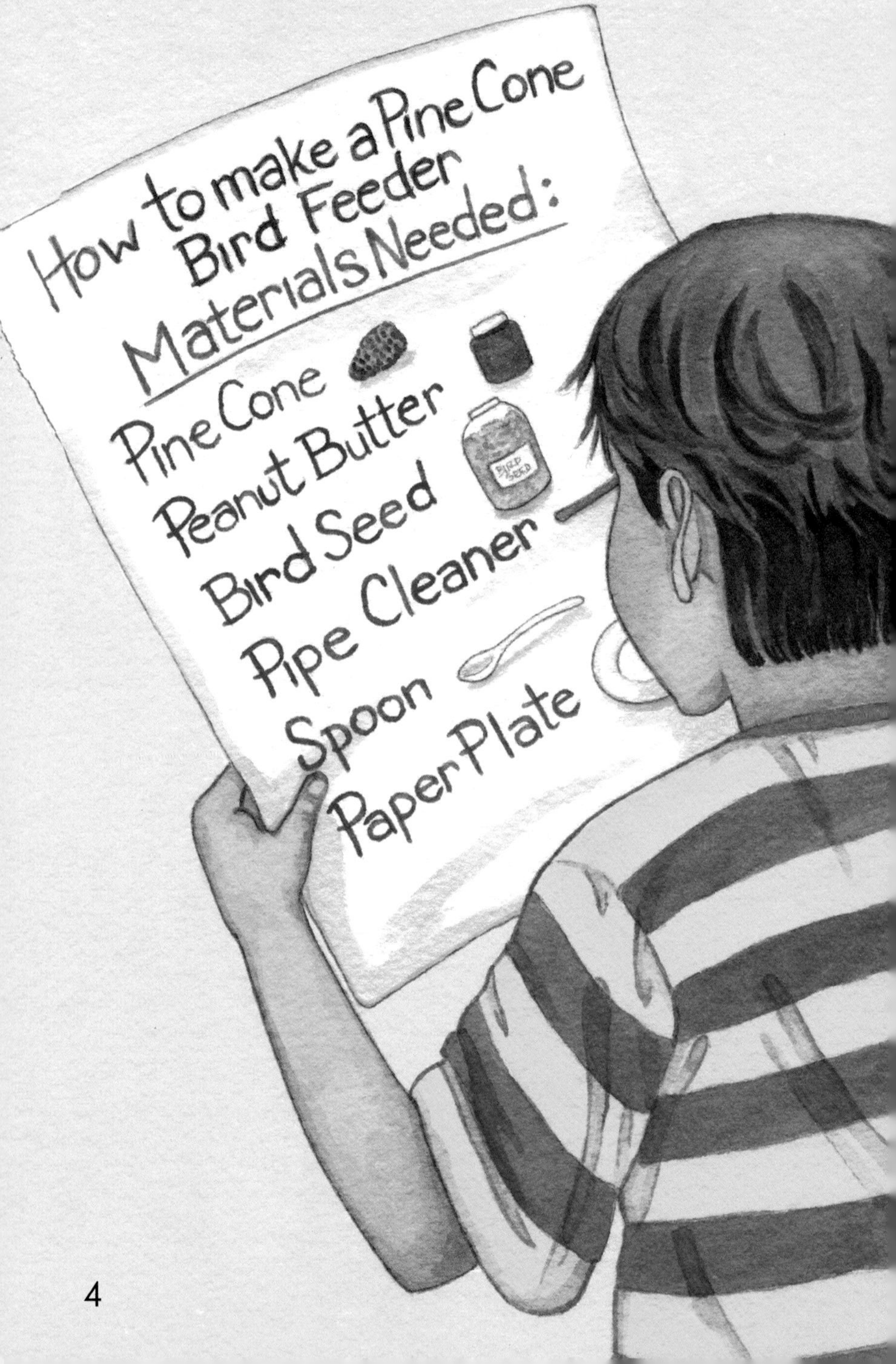

How to make a Pine Cone Bird Feeder

Materials Needed:

- Pine Cone
- Peanut Butter
- Bird Seed
- Pipe Cleaner
- Spoon
- Paper Plate

"I'll get the plates and pine cones," said Jake. He counted out four paper plates for his group and carefully placed four pine cones on top of them. "Ouch! These pine cones are prickly."

"I'll get the pipe cleaners," said Kim. "Here are brown pipe cleaners for all of you and a purple one for me. My feeder will be the best one."

"I can't wait to eat some of this!" Robert said as he picked up a jar of peanut butter and four spoons.

"It's not for you," said Maria. "It's for the birds." She picked up a jar of bird seed and carried it to the table.

The children read the instructions.

Steps to Make a Pine Cone
Bird Feeder:

1. Wrap the pipe cleaner around
   the large end of the pine cone.

2. Twist the ends of the pipe
   cleaner together to make a
   hanger for the bird feeder.

"I did it," said Robert. He held up his
pine cone. "Can I eat some peanut
butter now?"

"No," said Maria. "We have five more
steps to do!"

The children read:

3. Use the back of the spoon to spread peanut butter all over the pine cone.

"Good," said Jake as he smothered his pine cone with peanut butter. "That will cover the prickles."

Kim poked peanut butter deep inside the pine cone. "This way the birds get more food. My feeder will be the best one."

The next step said:

**4. Pour bird seed onto the paper plate.**

Jake picked up the jar and poured some seeds onto his plate. He passed the jar to Maria.

Maria poured. She passed the jar to Robert.

Robert poured. He passed the jar to Kim.

Kim poured. "Hey, there's not enough left!" When Jake wasn't looking, she switched plates with him.

The next step said:

5. Roll the pine cone in the bird seed until it is covered.

The children rolled.

Kim used her spoon to pour extra bird seed deep into the pine cone. "My feeder will be the best one," she said.

"I ran out of bird seed," said Jake.

"Here, Jake," said Robert. "You can have some of mine." He handed Jake his plate. Then he licked his spoon.

13

The last steps said:

6. Hang your bird feeder from a
   tree branch.

7. Watch the birds come for their
   winter snack!

The children went outside to hang their
feeders.

"They're so pretty," said Maria.

"Mine's the best," said Kim.

They went inside and watched through
the window. "Look!" said Maria.

"Oh, no!" said Kim.

"Ha, ha," laughed Robert.

"You're right, Kim," said Jake. "Your feeder is the best. It's not the best *bird* feeder, though . . . it's the best *squirrel* feeder!"